GO
GIRL!

BACK TO SCHOOL

GO TO

WWW.MYGOGIRLSERIES.COM

FOR **FREE** GO GIRL! DOWNLOADS,
QUIZZES, READING CLUB GUIDES,
AND LOTS MORE GO GIRL! FUN.

JUL 10

CH

Get to know the girls of

#1 THE SECRET CLUB

#2 THE WORST GYMNAST

#3 SISTER SPIRIT

#4 LUNCHTIME RULES

#5 SLEEPOVER!

#6 SURF'S UP!

#7 DANCING QUEEN

#8 CATCH ME IF YOU CAN

#9 THE NEW GIRL

#10 BASKETBALL BLUES

#11 CAMP CHAOS

#12 BACK TO SCHOOL